How To Make A Star

And

The World Ended

LIANA BROOKS

OTHER WORKS

ALL I WANT FOR CHRISTMAS

All I Want For Christmas Is A Reaper
All I Want For Christmas Is A Werewolf

FLEET OF MALIK

Bodies In Motion
Change of Momentum

HEROES AND VILLAINS

Even Villains Fall In Love
Even Villains Go To The Movies
Even Villains Have Interns
Even Villains Play The Hero (books 1 – 3 omnibus)
The Polar Terror

TIME AND SHADOWS

The Day Before
Convergence Point
Decoherence

SHORTER WORKS

Fey Lights
Prime Sensations
Darkness and Good

Find other works by the author at www.lianabrooks.com

How To Make A Star and

The World Ended

INKLET #92

LIANA BROOKS

Inkprint PRESS
www.inkprintpress.com

Copyright © 2022 Liana Brooks

All rights reserved. No part of this book may be reproduced in any form or by any electronic or mechanical means, including information storage and retrieval systems, without permission in writing from the publisher, except by a reviewer, who may quote brief passages in a review.

This is a work of fiction. All characters, organisations and events are the author's creation, or are used fictitiously.

Print ISBN: 978-1-922434-32-6
eBook ISBN: 9798201748654

www.inkprintpress.com

National Library of Australia Cataloguing-in-Publication Data
Brooks, Liana 1982 –
How To Make A Star and The World Ended
36 p.
ISBN: 978-1-922434-32-6
Inkprint Press, Canberra, Australia
1. Fiction—Fairy Tales, Folk Tales, Legends & Mythology
2. Fiction—Fantasy—General 3. Fiction—Science Fiction—General 4. Fiction—Short Stories

First Print Edition: October 2022
Cover photo © Sergey Nivens via Deposit Photos
Cover design © Inkprint Press
Interior art © Amy Laurens

HOW TO MAKE A STAR[1]

'Make a classic, five-pointed star with two pieces of origami paper and a piece of tape!'

Easy, anyone can make a star. It says so right in the book.

One piece of blue paper shimmering like the summer sky. One piece as

---

[1] Annotated by Yours Truly with Helpful Hints to avoid certain destruction of the universe and other Regrettable Incidents.

black as winter night, cold and limitless.

1 – Using a square piece of paper, turn it so it looks like a diamond. If the paper is colored on one side, have the colored sided facing up.

The black paper sits on the desk like a sulky, teenage blackhole, radiating malevolence and rejection of all authority.[2] There. One step closer to stars burning brightly overhead.

2 – Fold two tips together to form a tidy triangle. The color should be hidden.

Absolutely no problems there. Triangle ACHIEVED. Black and sinister looking because the paper is black on both sides, but very triangular.

---

[2] In retrospect this should have been A Clue.

Two acute angles. One obtuse. With a certain, rugged hint of mountain. This is a triangle with purpose. With a destiny.

3 – Take the left edge of the triangle and fold it to the top edge.

The directions said nothing about this, but humming *The Grand 'Ol Duke Of York* seems appropriate.[3]

4 – Turn the paper over.

Look! Almost done. This is almost a star! It's so exciting. It looks even darker than before.

---

[3] At the time. Perhaps something by REM would have been more appropriate.

Let the record show that the end of the world was not due for at least another millennia and therefore Yours Truly cannot be blamed for any unplanned events hastening that great and dreadful day.

5 – Carefully bring the left corner to the right corner to fold the triangle in half…

This feels unexpectedly heavy. Was it supposed to be heavy?

…Your star will now look like the diagram in the book.

Ahh… All right, two triangles, a trapezoid flap, nothing about weight.
Wait. Where'd the other paper go? It was right here a moment ago.
What is pulling at my sleeve?
Oh. The black paper.
Well, that's fine then, stars have gravity, don't they? Perfectly normal. Odd that the book didn't mention it, but perhaps the writer thought it would be obvious.
Found the blue paper! It had fallen into the black one.
Not to worry, it's only slightly wrinkled. As long as the tape doesn't

go anywhere, this will be fine. No worries at all. Everything's perfectly as it should be. What's the next step?

6 – Pressing the flap open, press down to create a crease, making sure that the edges line up and the point remains sharp.

Sharp sounds a little… dangerous. Ah ha ha ha.
Ow.[4]

7 – Lay the second piece of paper down like a diamond, color side down.

Blue paper! We're saved!
Lovely, gentle, friendly blue paper with no sharp edges.

8 – Create a triangle by folding the bottom point to the top point and creating a firm crease.

---

[4] Note to Future Star Makers: stars hurt.

No trouble at all there. Blue triangle ACHIEVED. It's warping slightly because of the weight of the black half of the star.

But these things happen. Totally normal cosmic phenomenon. Utterly unremarkable.[5]

9 – Fold the triangle in half again.

It says nothing about using tape to secure anything at this point, but the gravity of the black half of the star is significant. The writer probably mean to say Step 0: Tape Yourself To the Floor. That's sensible. Let's do it now and call it Step 9.5.[6]

---

[5] A regrettable lack of foresight on the part of Yours Truly.

[6] Nowhere in the directions is a type of tape specified. From experience, Yours Truly recommends something stronger than 100,000,000 mile-an-hour tape.

10 – Turn the triangle so there is a flat line on top and the sharp point is aimed at you.

That… That seems unwise.

11 – Place the first folded piece of paper next to the sharp triangle pointed at you.

…Um…

Maybe this needs a rethink. Stars are lovely and all. At a distance.

But, perhaps there's some danger in creating a star right here…

12 – Carefully place the sharp triangle between the two folded flaps of—[7]

"What happened?"
"Well, I was trying to make a star."

---

[7] Oops.

"A star?"

"Yes."

"And you made—"

"—a black hole that devoured the universe. Yes. The tape proved problematic in the last step."

"This is like the cake incident all over again!"[8]

"It is not. There was no baking of any kind. What? Don't look at me like that! The book said this was an easy project for all ages!"

"Oh, it took all ages. From Day One of the universe straight to Kaboom!"

"Stars can be temperamental. You know that. Really, it was a tiny little accident. A missed crease. I know exactly what I did wrong! I'll fix it. Don't worry."

"Oh, very well. Just see you put it back right this time. I swear there

---

[8] The directions were very easy to misread.

was something off about that last version."[9]

"You'll never know the difference. Promise."

"Are the cupcakes done?"

"...Oh. Dear. I knew I'd forgotten something."[10]

---

[9] Admit nothing. Deny everything. Remember, when the universe has exploded no one has proof about anything.

[10] Poor, burnt cupcakes.

THE WORLD ENDED[11]

"So... the world ended?"

"Um, yes. Sorry about that." There was a nervous silence. "If it helps, I think I know where I went wrong."

"Really?"

"Yes! Well... probably. There's one or six places where things went a little off track. It won't happen again. Probably."

"There's no world for it to *happen* in again."

---

[11] Definitely nothing to do with the cake incident. Absolutely not.

"Yes, like I said, minor oversight. Completely fixable."

"What? You're just going to wave a hand and bring everything back?"

"Er, not as such. No. But I can start over. Use different molecules this time. Something less combustible. Iron maybe. Or helium."

"But… Will they have donuts?"

"Oh, definitely. Every reality has donuts, don't worry about that."

"Right then."

"Right."

"But no more baking, understood? Next time you have to buy my birthday cake."

"Absolutely. Once I restart all life, I will leave the cooking completely up to whatever evolves from the muck."

"Good. Thank you."

THE MAKING OF *HOW TO MAKE A STAR* AND *THE WORLD ENDED*

If you read this in the voice of Michael Sheen or David Tennant you fully understand where this story came from. You know. SUBTLE HINTS R US.

These stories exist solely for my own amusement because I could see how things could go wrong. Really wrong. And that amuses me.

It probably shouldn't.

But it does.

Enjoy!

Read more by Liana Brooks!

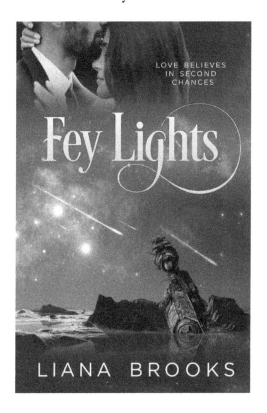

FEY LIGHTS

Dark water writhed over the ship's deck, a living thing hunting for prey, stinging like acid where it touched bare skin. Jeani stumbled over the guts of her ship, swearing in every language she knew. Her foot fell through a hole in the deck created by the crash. Hot metal gouged her leg as tears ran down her cheeks.

I don't want to die like this. There has to be a way out.

There is *a way out. The same way the water is coming in.*

Running was out of the question. Half-limping, half-swimming through the rising water, Jeani forced herself back to the rear of the ship, navigating by touch and the weak glow of the emergency lights that hadn't burst, back to the gaping wound that was once the engine room and secondary hold. Pressure from the rapid descent into the gravity well and the gushing water warped the frame, creating a strong current. Jeani grabbed the free-fall handle near the emergency door and pressed her free hand to the glowing lock.

Nothing.

She tried yanking the override.

Nothing.

She kicked the door with her good leg.

Pressure sent the door flying inwards at the head of a tidal wave. Jeani gasped for air and went under. Seconds ticked away as she grappled blindly for the next free-fall handle, the current tugging at her.

The hand-hold slipped out of her grip. She pushed up once, bumping her head against the high ceiling of the engine room as she gasped for air. The current swirled under her, pulling her down into the darkness.

Saltwater stung her face. She shuddered as something nipped at her bleeding leg. Ignoring the pain, she clawed at the water until she broke through and gasped in the alien atmosphere. Water crashed over her in the darkness.

Rough, warm sand rubbed against her skin. Sucking in a lungful of the oxygen-rich air, Jeani flipped onto her stomach and pulled herself away from the water. It lapped at her legs, a wayward lover begging her to return.

She laughed as she looked at the strange stars overhead. Her lungs burned, her leg ached, she was shaking with delayed shock, but she was alive. "See, Hothi, I told you I wasn't going to die that easy."

Dominique pushed through the crowd and looked down at the beach.

"Could be a Lander," Gregor said as he adjusted his cap. "Saw the prison ships sailing past this last moon. Could be a Lander," he repeated with a final snort.

A knife waved past Dominique's face, stabbing toward the figure on the beach. "'Twere wedding lights last night. Lit up the sky with fire, set the trees to burning," said Beau.

"'Tain't no fire touched the trees. Trees are fine," Gregor argued. "'Tis a Lander."

"Fey fire," someone said behind him. "Fey burn things with cold fire." A fist hit Dominique's shoulder. "Fey can turn a man's bones to ice. They summon monsters from the deep."

One of the women crossed her fingers and made the sign of the arch to ward off the ill will of the deep dwellers.

"Landers bring plague," Adrian said grimly. He too tapped Dominique's shoulder. "We can't let a Lander near the village."

"We's best shooting it from here," Gregor said.

Another shook his head. "Arrows can't touch fey."

"You volunteering to go down there to slit its throat?" Gregor demanded.

"Such a thing to ask a man! I've got kin, I have."

There was the sound of shuffling feet. A cool sea breeze wrapped around Dominique's legs as the crowd parted. He filled their silence with imagined conversations.

"He's a Lander," one would say in the Silent way of the island-born. *"Got no kin nor woman of his own, does he,"* someone else would murmur.

Dominique kept the snarl he felt forming in his throat from escaping.

"Will you go?" Adrian whispered, confirming his suspicions. "None will make you, if you say no."

"You'll go?" Dominique asked with a half-smile. Adrian wasn't a bad man. Island born, birthed in the sea, born running on the beach and listening to the waves.

The island-born claimed the waves spoke back to those that listened. The saltwater seeped into their blood so they could hear the thoughts of others like they heard the song of the ocean. Like all the island born, Adrian had no trouble believing every infamy laid against the Landers who lived on the far side of the ocean, in the land of the tyrant.

Adrian shrugged. "Better to slit the Lander's throat on the beach than let it breathe on a child in the village. We'll all die of black blood and fever before the tide is high."

"I'll go," Dominique said, loud enough for his voice to carry to the back of the crowd. "I'll go see to the Lander. I'll send him down to the docks in the south. He can find work there if he likes."

"What if it be fey?" Gregor asked, eyes wide.

Dominique studied the lone figure on the distant sand below, a sad creature sprawled under the hot morning sun. "The fey have a treaty with the Tyrant of Urull. The first tyrant traded his soul for the secrets of the fey lights—wedding lights," he corrected himself, using the island-born term. "The first tyrant lost his mind when the fey showed him the wonders of their world. Men that could turn into dogs. Deep monsters that could walk as men. Women so beautiful that they could suck the soul of a man as he walked past, steal his life with a kiss.

"The tyrants all have made a pact

with the fey, traded their subjects to the fey for their favor, but they've never let the fey roam the lands. No fey walk outside the tyrant's gates in Urull. No fey step on the white sands of the islands."

"Maybe this one is outcast," Beau said. "A prisoner, like all the other Landers sent here."

"You've got a leak in your hull," Adrian said, punching Beau in the arm. "You think the tyrant could make a prisoner out of the fey? You think a man could keep one of them under lock and key?"

"But... wedding lights!" Beau looked to Dominique for support. "The lights haven't touched our sky in years."

"No one's been out walking in years," Dominique said. "Who was out last night?" He turned and scanned the crowd.

Hardy folk, the island-born. They

wore homespun cloth, britches of old sail cloth traded from down the coast, filigree gold necklaces twined around shells and sea gems. All of them came from Lander families at some point in their history, Landers who had either escaped the tyrants, or been banished to a slow death on the distant islands, depending on who you asked.

But the islands were in their blood now. They spoke in Silence, and left him an outcast. The women looked away from him, the older men met his gaze, and one boy blushed. "Tris? Were you out walking last night?"

The boy with dark eyes and a thatch of red hair looked up. "May have been. What's it to you?"

Someone chuckled.

"Explains the wedding lights," Gregor muttered. "You still ought to slit the throat first. That one's not going to give you any answer you'll be wanting."

Keep reading! Head to www.inkprintpress.com/lianabrooks/feylights/ to buy your copy now!

ABOUT THE AUTHOR

Liana Brooks loves big dogs, cheerful children, and a job that allows her to be home more often than not. When she isn't traveling, she enjoys writing science fiction in every form, from sprawling space operas romances (the *Fleet of Malik* series, starting with *Bodies In Motion*), to the antics of a super-powered family (the *Heroes and Villains* series, which can be read in any order), to intricate time-travel murder mysteries (the *Time And Shadow* series, starting with *The Day Before*).

Liana also maintains a soft spot for paranormal romances. She writes the popular *All I Want For Christmas* novellas, including *All I Want For Christmas Is A Werewolf* and *All I Want For Christmas Is A Reaper*.

You can learn more about her and her books at www.LianaBrooks.com.

INKLETS

Collect them all! Released on the 1st and 15th of each month.

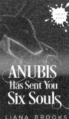